Lunar Mooner Lula Learns:

A Few Life Lessons That Aren't Just for The Birds

Written and Illustrated by

Tarri N. Driver

MW00952980

Lunar Mooner Lula Learns:
A Few Life Lessons That Aren't Just for The Birds

Copyright © 2017 by Tarri N. Driver

www.lunarmoonerlula.com

MCP Books
2301 Lucien Way #415
Maitland, FL 32751
407·339·4217
www.MCPBooks.com

All rights reserved. No part of this publication may be reproduced, stored in a retrieval system, or transmitted, in any form or by any means, electronic, mechanical, photocopying, recording, or otherwise, without the prior written permission of the author.

ISBN-13: 978-1-63505-433-0
Distributed by Itasca Books

Illustrations by Tarri Driver
Edited by Christopher J. Driver

First Edition, 2016.

Printed in the United States of America

Written and Illustrated by Tarri N. Driver

I have to get out of here
I just can't take it!

Lula wonders
what begins where the sidewalk ends.

6

"Well,
Helloooo!
And whooooo
might
youuuuu be?"

asks a voice from
the trees.

Lula gasps.

"Are you lost?

Where are you going?

Are you looking for something?"

Lula is not sure how to answer...

...but she *is* sure she must go forward...

...even if she is a little scared...

11

Lula begins to relax.

She notices

Generous birds

Collaborative birds

A Bold bird

Cooperative birds

a Discerning bird

Content birds

A Patient bird

23

Taking a moment, Lula notices how relaxed and calm she feels. Her mind is clear, and her heart is joyful.

Lula decides

her thoughts, words
and actions will be brighter,
every day.

Until next time...

Thank You

Flower Child (SCK), for your hours and hours of help, advice and creative input (I know there was sweat, and there were tears too). Liz, (LCA) for your advice and creative input, and for pushing me to swallow my pride and accept your sister's help, for goodness sake! PB and JS for the crazy helpful studio session. All my friends and family who gave me so much support, encouragement and love over the eons this book has been percolating. My Momma for giving me gentle reminders to keep on keeping on. My Papa for saying to me over the years, "I'm telling you, Sissy, you should really do something with that Lula character." My husband (partner in crime, collaborator, editor-in-chief, constructive critic) for being brutally honest, patient, loving and steadfast. You make me a better me. I couldn't have done this without you. Lastly but mostly, THANK YOU sweet Jesus! This baby has finally been birthed.

About the Author/Illustrator:

Tarri N. Driver majored in fine arts, with an emphasis on painting and a minor in psychology. She then earned a master's degree in education with a focus on expressive therapies. For a decade she worked as a board-certified, registered art therapist, licensed professional counselor and mental health services provider in inner-city schools and a children's hospital before taking a hiatus from the mental health field to focus on her own art. Her unique experiences as an artist and therapist have influenced the roots of this story and the Lula character's genesis and evolution. Throughout her life, Tarri has been a visual artist in some capacity. She uses whatever she has on hand to create her artwork. Paints, inks, clementine boxes, *National Geographic* magazines, old photos and fabric scraps are a few of her favorite materials. She's recently moved to the scenic hills of East Tennessee with her ridiculously supportive husband, Chris Driver, and she has rediscovered the joy and madness of oil painting. She's heavily influenced by humor and absurdity, and Jungian and Gestalt theory. See more of her work at www.lunarmoonerlula.com.

About the Editor:

Christopher J. Driver has the loyalty of a saint, the intensity of a Carolina Reaper and a deliciously dry, wry wit. He wrote his master's thesis on the science fiction films *Blade Runner* and *Solaris*. He feels that *Planes, Trains and Automobiles* and *Grosse Pointe Blank* are significantly underappreciated. He has recently published his first book, a darkly comic memoir: **HARDBARNED!** *One Man's Quest for Meaningful Work in the American South*, illustrated by Tarri. Follow his continuing adventures and random observations at www.hardbarned.com.